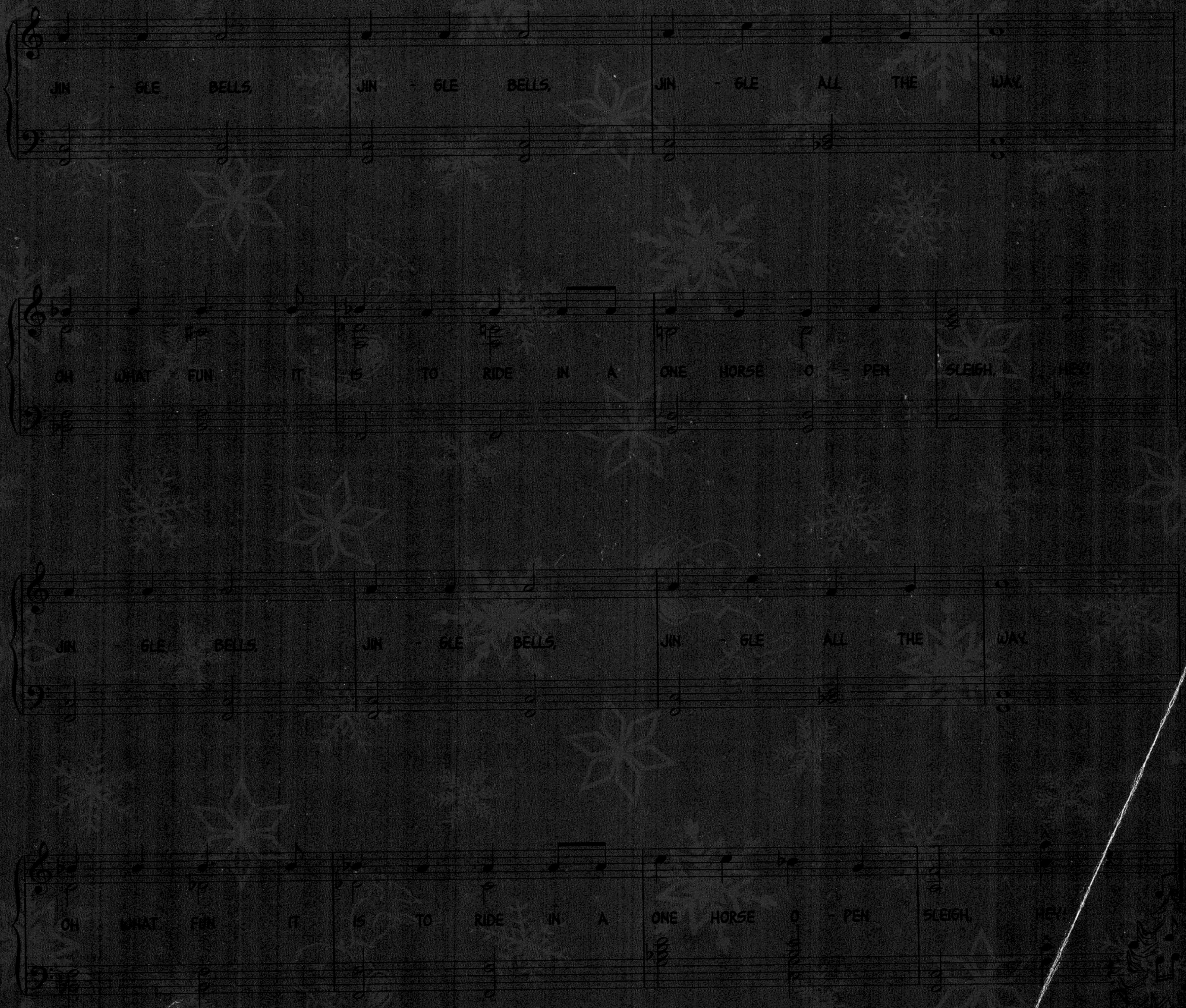
JIN - GLE BELLS, JIN - GLE BELLS, JIN - GLE ALL THE WAY.
OH WHAT FUN IT IS TO RIDE IN A ONE HORSE O - PEN SLEIGH, HEY!
JIN - GLE BELLS, JIN - GLE BELLS, JIN - GLE ALL THE WAY.
OH WHAT FUN IT IS TO RIDE IN A ONE HORSE O - PEN SLEIGH. HEY!

This Book Belongs To

_____

A Charlie Brown Christmas

SIMON SPOTLIGHT

An imprint of Simon & Schuster Children's Publishing Division
1230 Avenue of the Americas, New York, New York 10020
This Simon Spotlight edition September 2017
© 2017 Peanuts Worldwide LLC
For information about special discounts for bulk purchases, please contact Simon & Schuster
Special Sales at 1-866-506-1949 or business@simonandschuster.com.
Manufactured in China 0717 SCP
2 4 6 8 10 9 7 5 3 1
ISBN 978-1-5344-0455-7
ISBN 978-1-5344-0456-4 (eBook)

PEANUTS®

A Charlie Brown
Christmas

By Charles M. Schulz
Based on the animated special, the text was adapted by Maggie Testa
Illustrated by Vicki Scott

Simon Spotlight
New York   London   Toronto   Sydney   New Delhi

Christmastime was here. Soft snowflakes floated down from the sky, the sweet sound of carols filled the air, and everyone felt happy. Well, almost everyone . . .

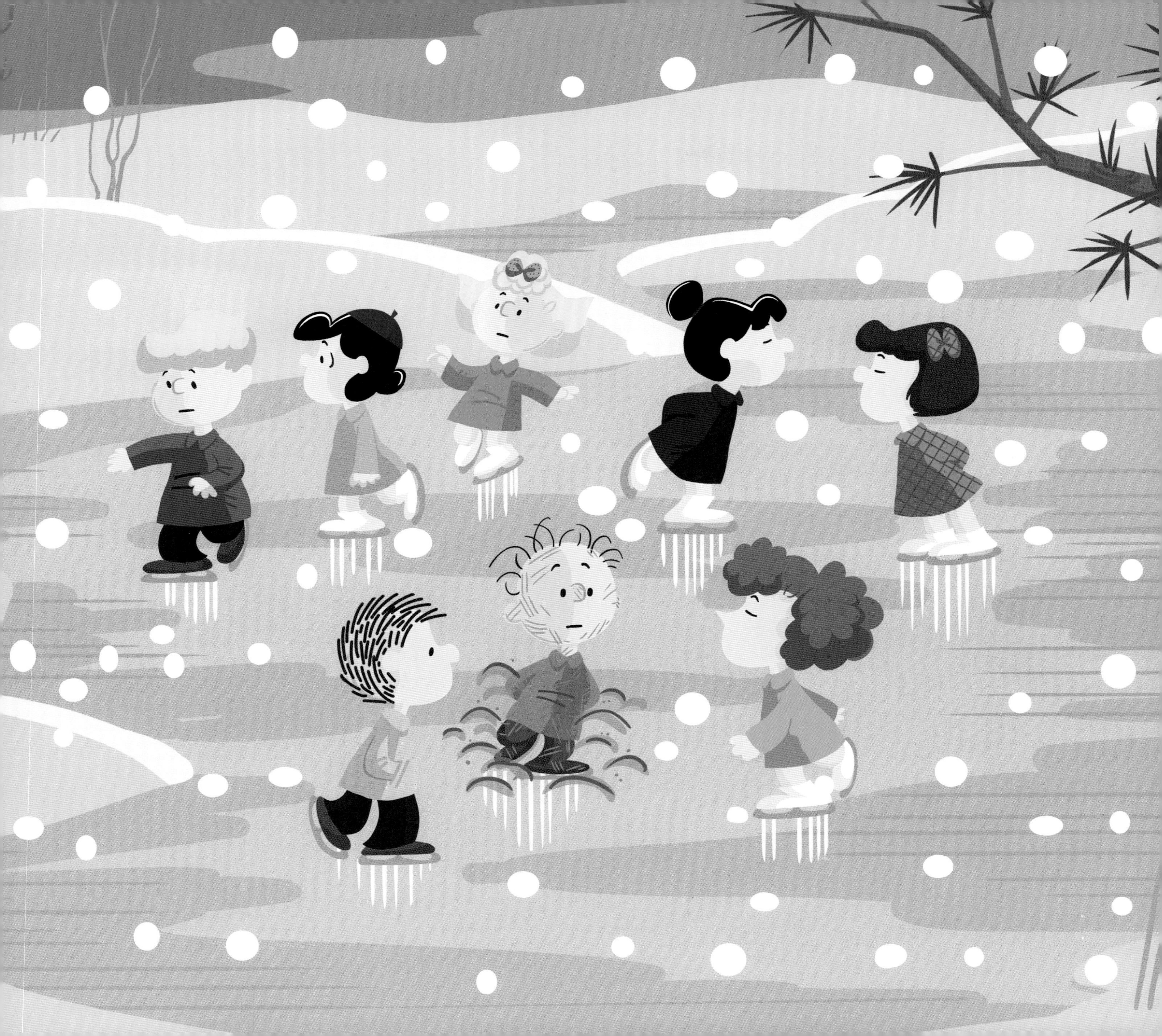

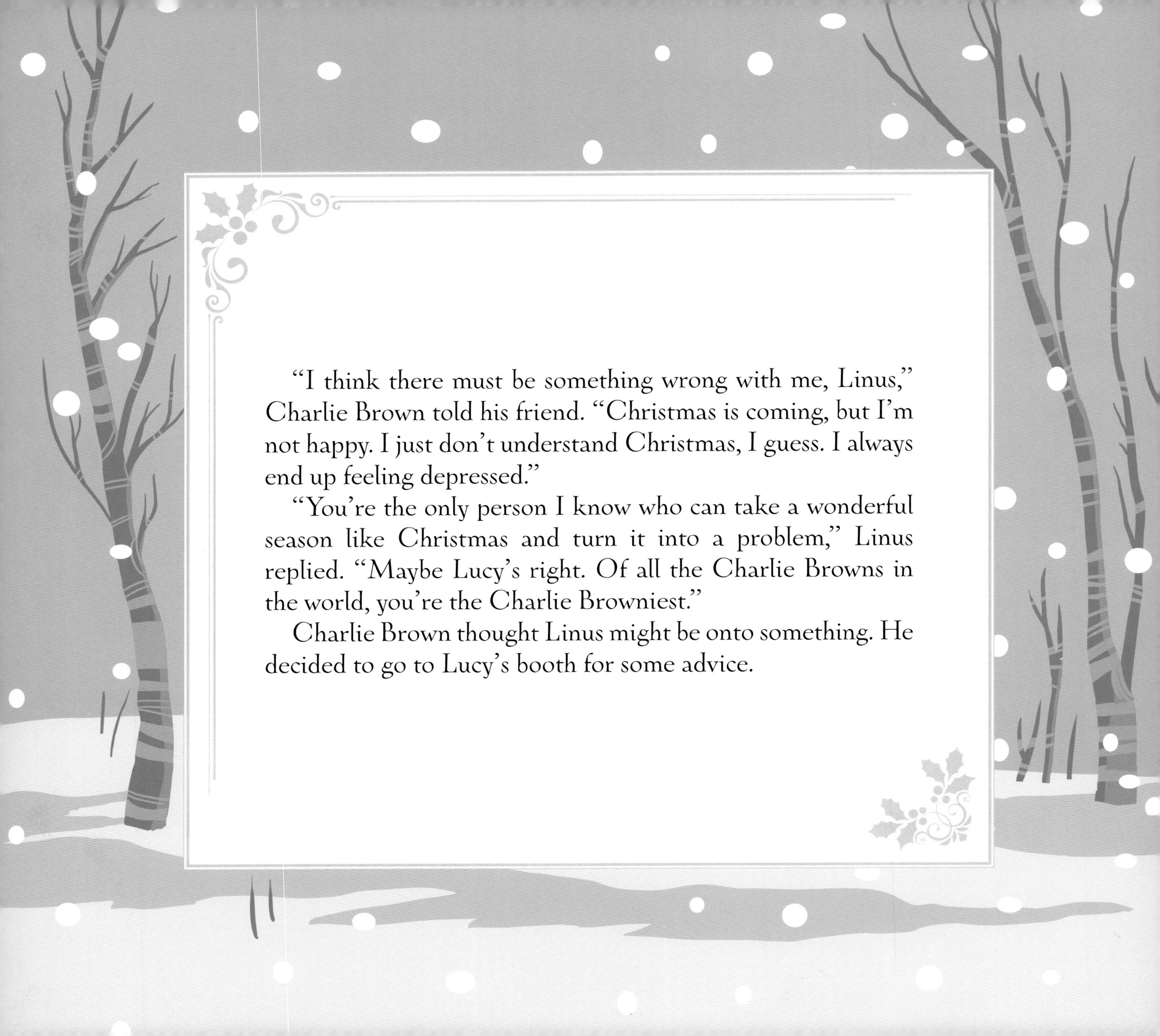

"I think there must be something wrong with me, Linus," Charlie Brown told his friend. "Christmas is coming, but I'm not happy. I just don't understand Christmas, I guess. I always end up feeling depressed."

"You're the only person I know who can take a wonderful season like Christmas and turn it into a problem," Linus replied. "Maybe Lucy's right. Of all the Charlie Browns in the world, you're the Charlie Browniest."

Charlie Brown thought Linus might be onto something. He decided to go to Lucy's booth for some advice.

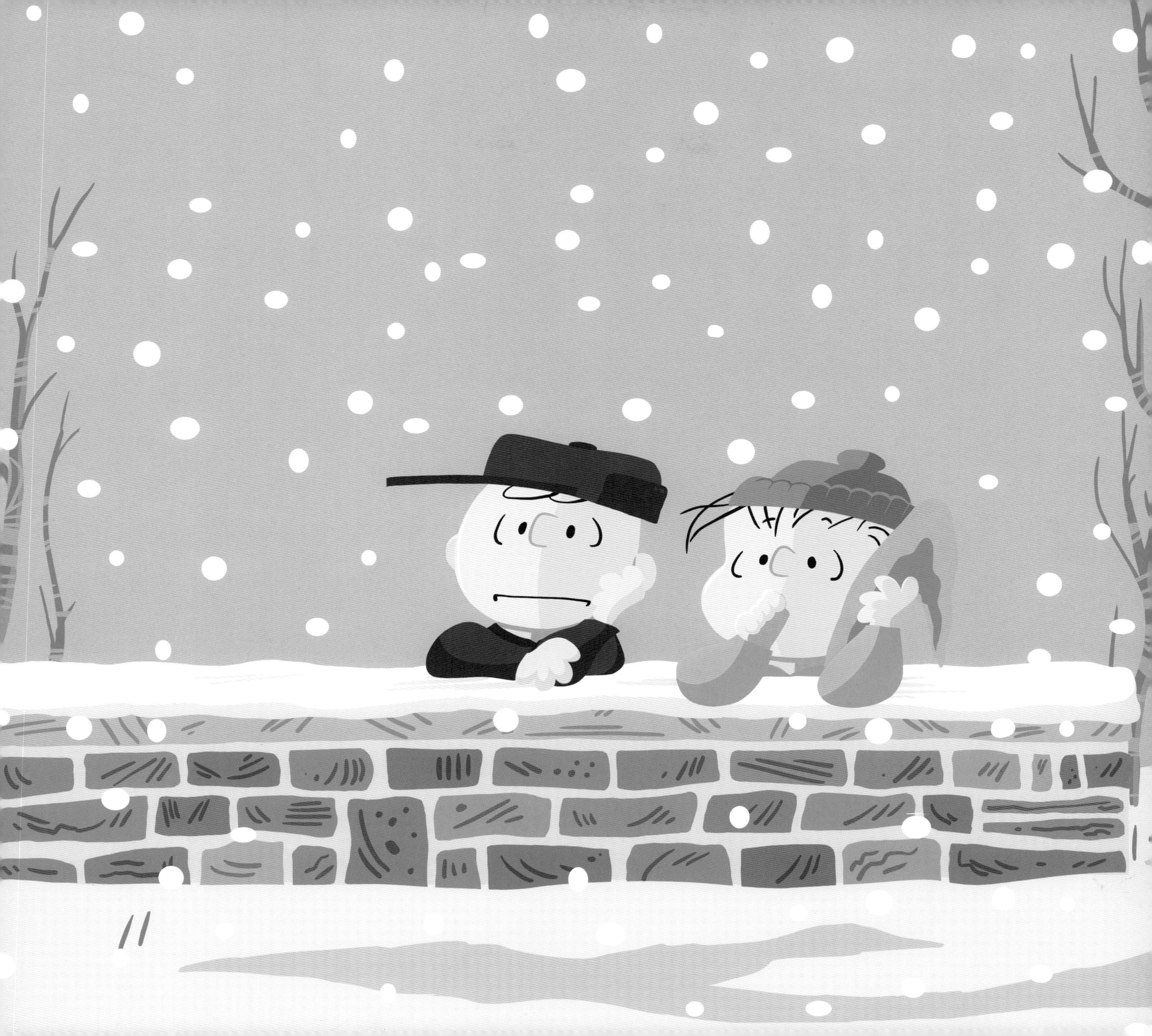

"Five cents, please," Lucy greeted him.

Charlie Brown dropped a nickel into Lucy's can.

Lucy shook the can. "I love hearing the beautiful sound of cold hard cash. Now, what seems to be your trouble?"

"I feel depressed," Charlie Brown told her.

"I think we'd better pinpoint your fears," said Lucy. "If we can find out what you're afraid of, we can label it. Are you afraid of staircases? If you are, then you have climacaphobia. Or maybe you have pantophobia."

"What's pantophobia?" asked Charlie Brown.

"The fear of everything," Lucy replied.

"That's it!" Charlie Brown cried out. He shouted so loudly that Lucy flew off her chair!

"Actually, Lucy, my trouble is Christmas," Charlie Brown admitted. "I just don't understand it. Instead of feeling happy, I feel sort of let down."

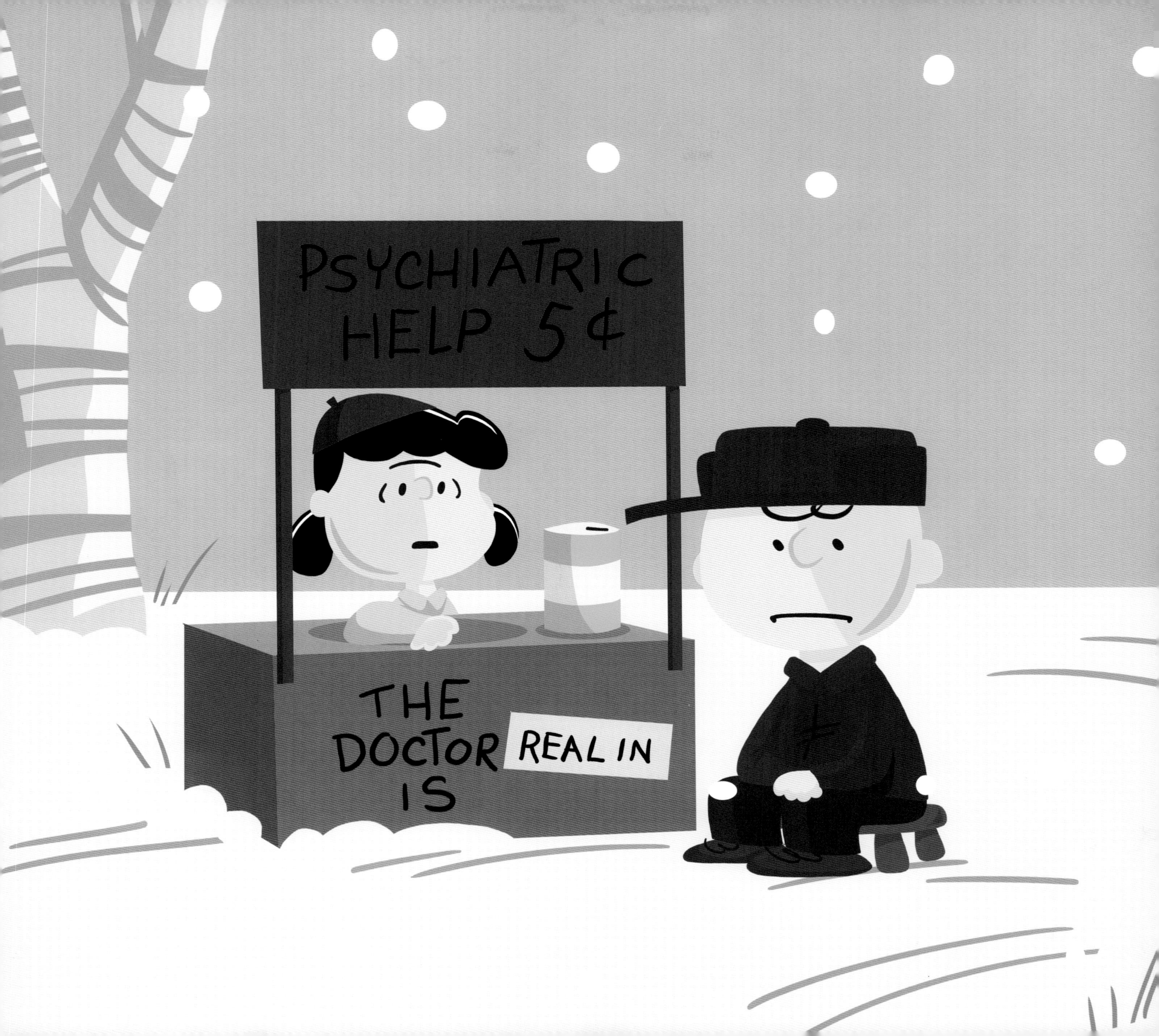
PSYCHIATRIC HELP 5¢
THE DOCTOR IS
REAL IN

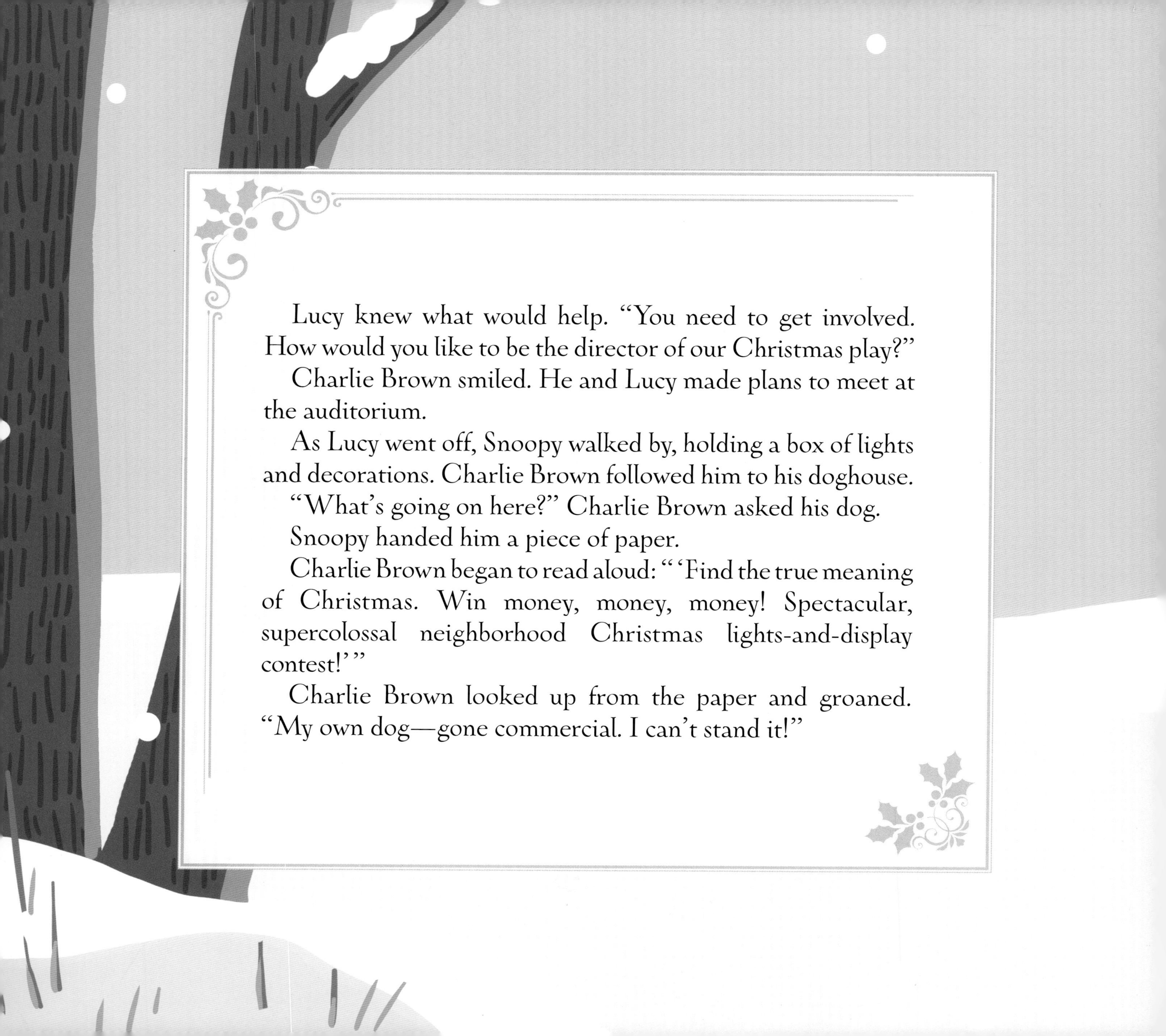

Lucy knew what would help. "You need to get involved. How would you like to be the director of our Christmas play?"

Charlie Brown smiled. He and Lucy made plans to meet at the auditorium.

As Lucy went off, Snoopy walked by, holding a box of lights and decorations. Charlie Brown followed him to his doghouse.

"What's going on here?" Charlie Brown asked his dog.

Snoopy handed him a piece of paper.

Charlie Brown began to read aloud: "'Find the true meaning of Christmas. Win money, money, money! Spectacular, supercolossal neighborhood Christmas lights-and-display contest!'"

Charlie Brown looked up from the paper and groaned. "My own dog—gone commercial. I can't stand it!"

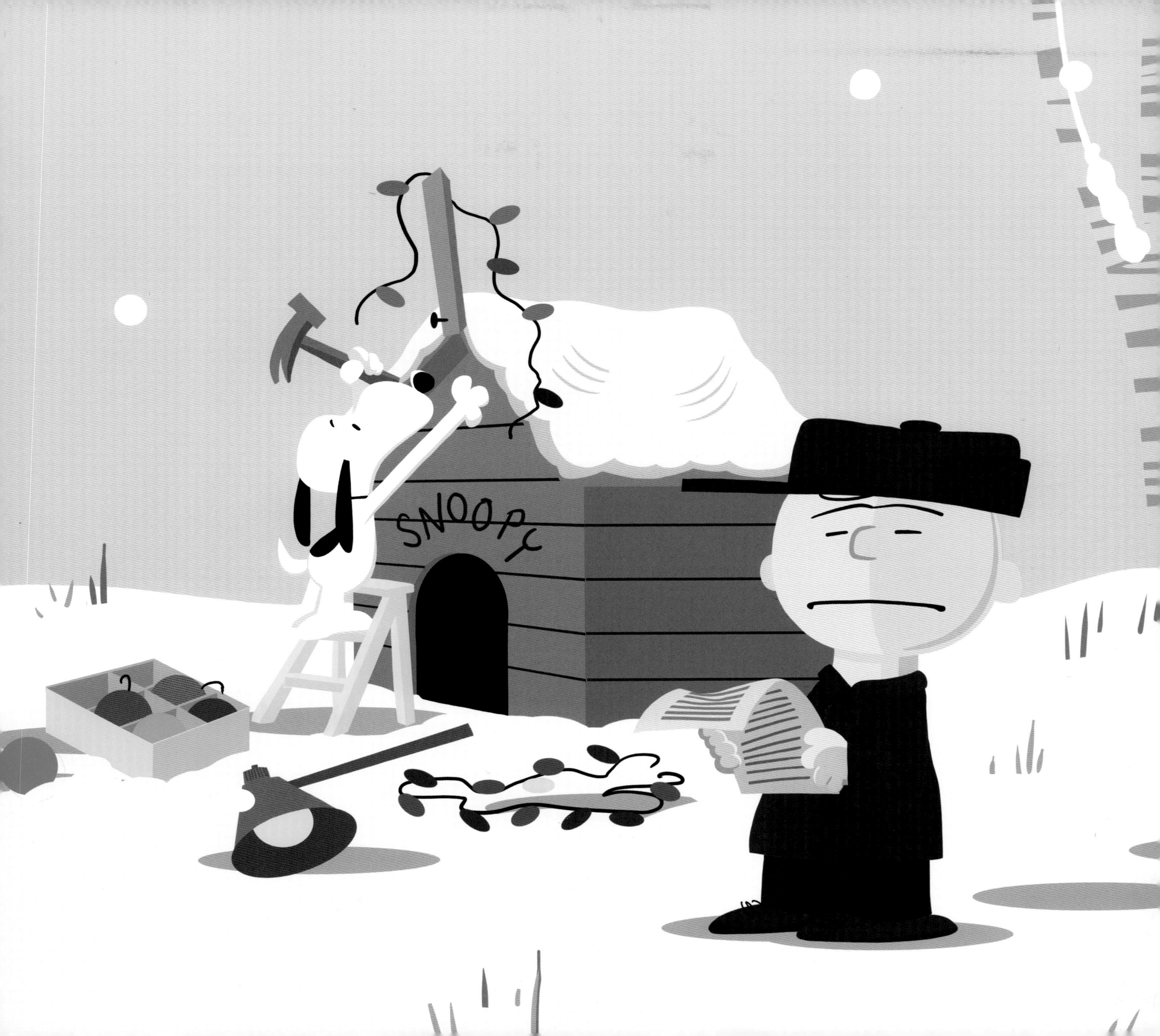
SNOOPY

Next, Charlie Brown ran into his sister, Sally.

"I've been looking for you, big brother. Will you please write a letter to Santa Claus for me?" Sally asked.

Sally began telling Charlie Brown what she wanted him to write: "Dear Santa Claus. How've you been? Did you have a nice summer? How is your wife? I have been extra good this year, so I have a long list of presents that I want. Please note the size and color of each item and send as many as possible. If it seems too complicated, make it easy on yourself. Just send money. How about tens and twenties?"

"Tens and twenties?" Charlie Brown cried. That didn't seem like the true Christmas spirit!

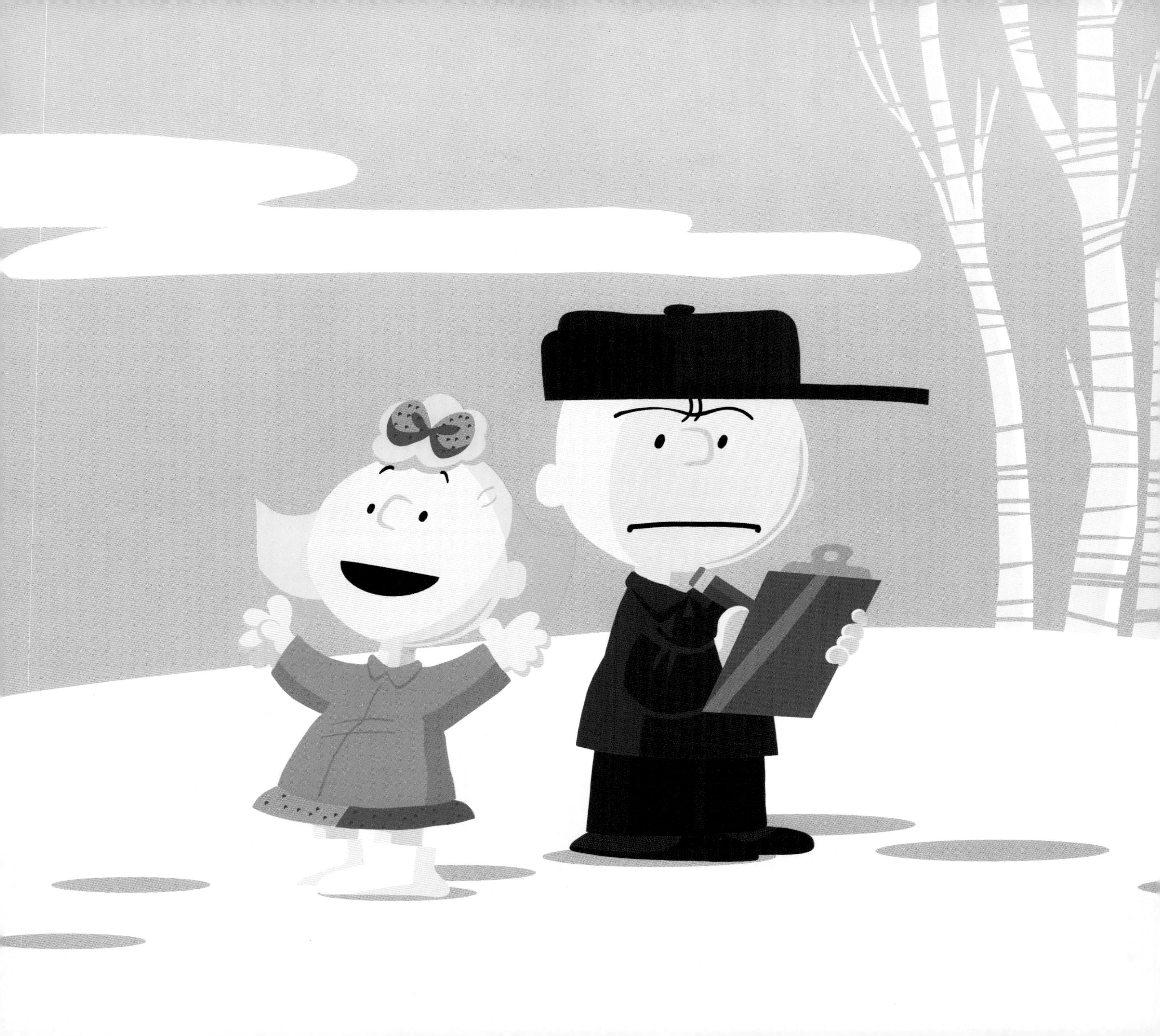

At the auditorium, Lucy had an announcement. "Quiet, everybody. Our director will be here any minute and we'll start rehearsal."

"Director? What director?" asked Patty.

"Charlie Brown," Lucy replied.

"Oh no! We're doomed!" said Violet.

"Here he comes!" said Lucy. "Attention, everyone!"

Charlie Brown addressed the cast, but no one listened to him. They were all dancing as Schroeder played his piano.

"Stop the music!" Charlie Brown shouted into his megaphone. "We're going to do this play, and we're going to do it right. Lucy, get those costumes and scripts and pass them out."

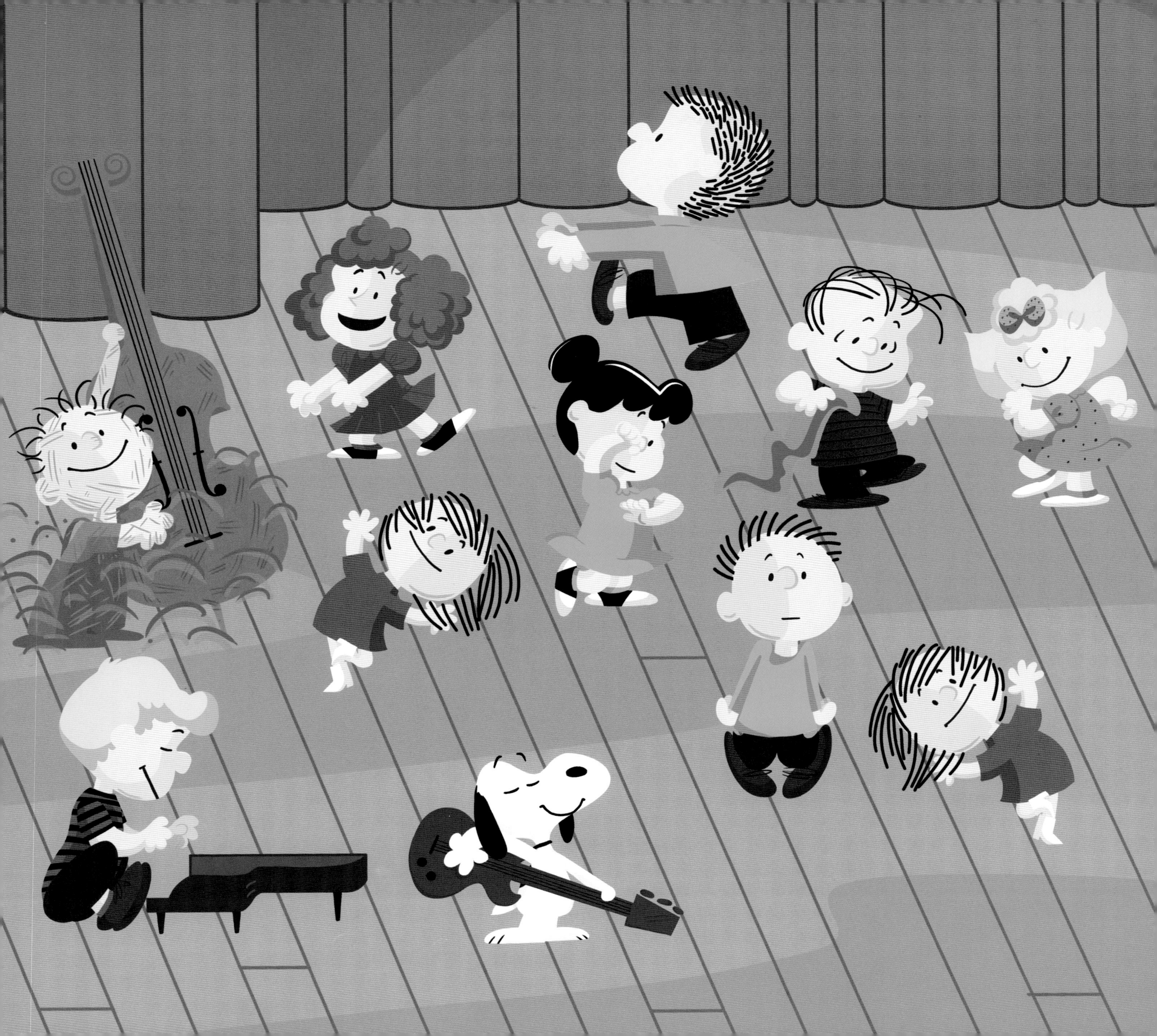

Lucy walked up to Frieda and gave her a script and a costume. "You're the innkeeper's wife."

"Did innkeepers' wives have naturally curly hair?" Frieda asked.

Lucy walked over to Pigpen. "You're the innkeeper."

Pigpen looked proud. "In spite of my outward appearance, I shall try to run a neat inn."

Lucy went over to Snoopy. "You'll have to be all the animals in our play," Lucy told him. "Can you be a sheep?"

"Baaaaaa!" bleated Snoopy.

"How about a cow?" asked Lucy.

"Moooo!" mooed Snoopy.

"How about a penguin?" asked Lucy.

"Clack, clack, clack!" Snoopy waddled around the stage.

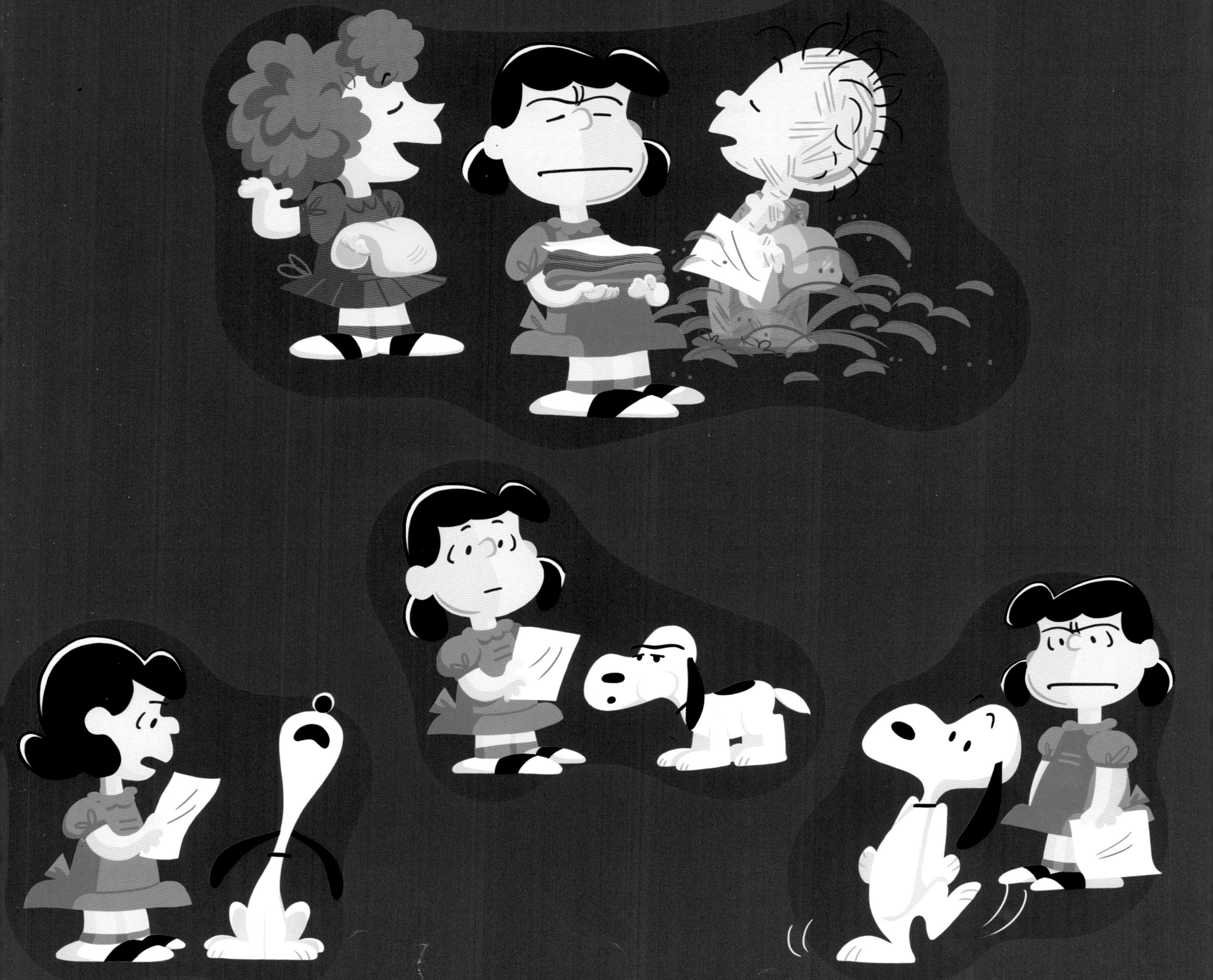

Soon, all the parts had been handed out and it was time for Charlie Brown to direct. He asked Schroeder to set the mood for the first scene. But as soon as Schroeder started playing, everyone started dancing again!

Lucy and Charlie Brown watched from the side of the stage.

"Isn't it a great play?" Lucy asked.

"It's all wrong," Charlie Brown told her.

"Let's face it. We all know that Christmas is a big commercial racket," Lucy said.

But Charlie Brown was determined. "Well, this is one play that's not going to be commercial."

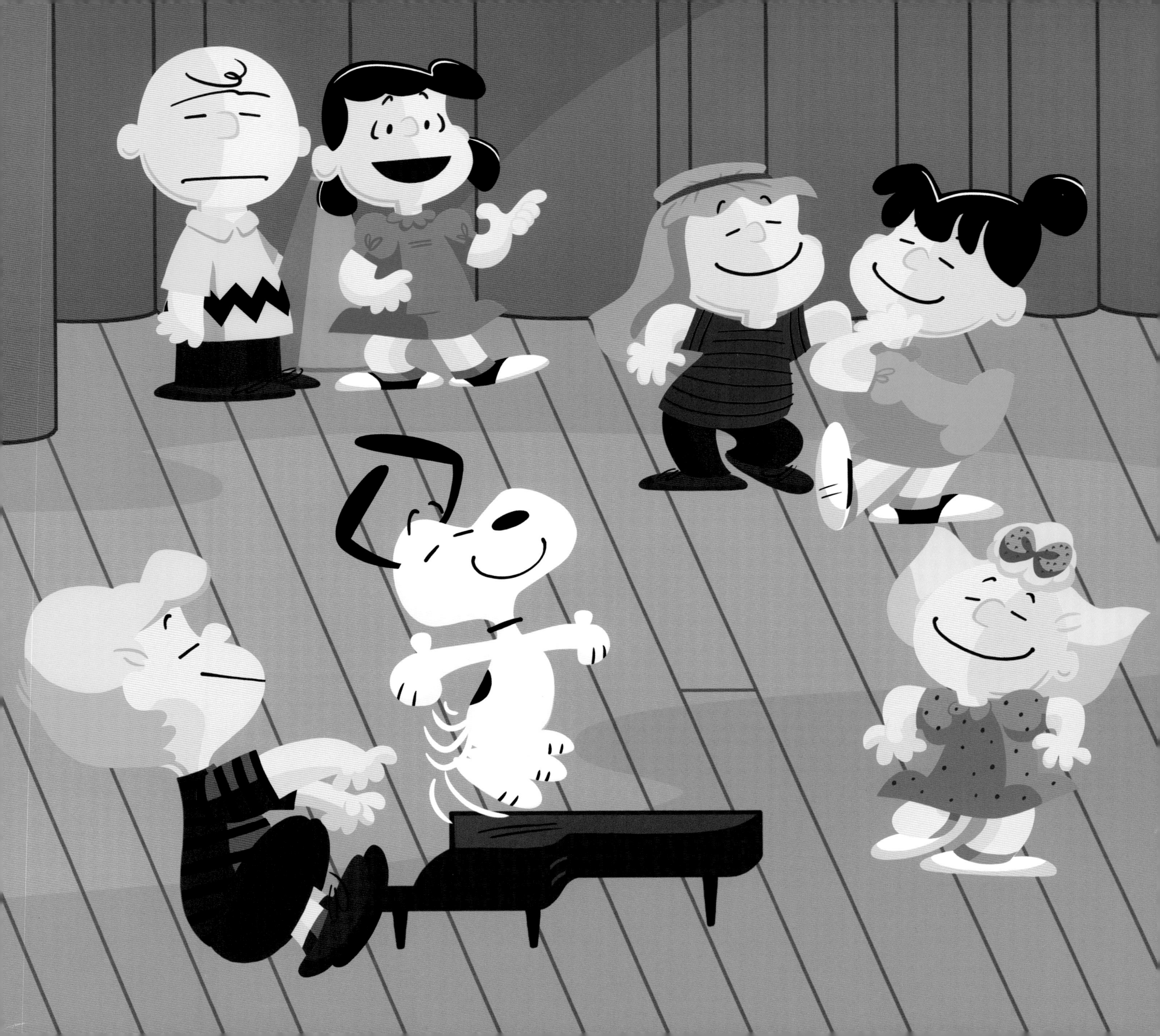

"What do you want?" Lucy asked.

"The proper mood," Charlie Brown responded. "We need a Christmas tree."

Lucy thought this was a great idea. "A great, big, shiny aluminum Christmas tree. That's it!"

"I'll take Linus with me," said Charlie Brown. "The rest of you, practice your lines."

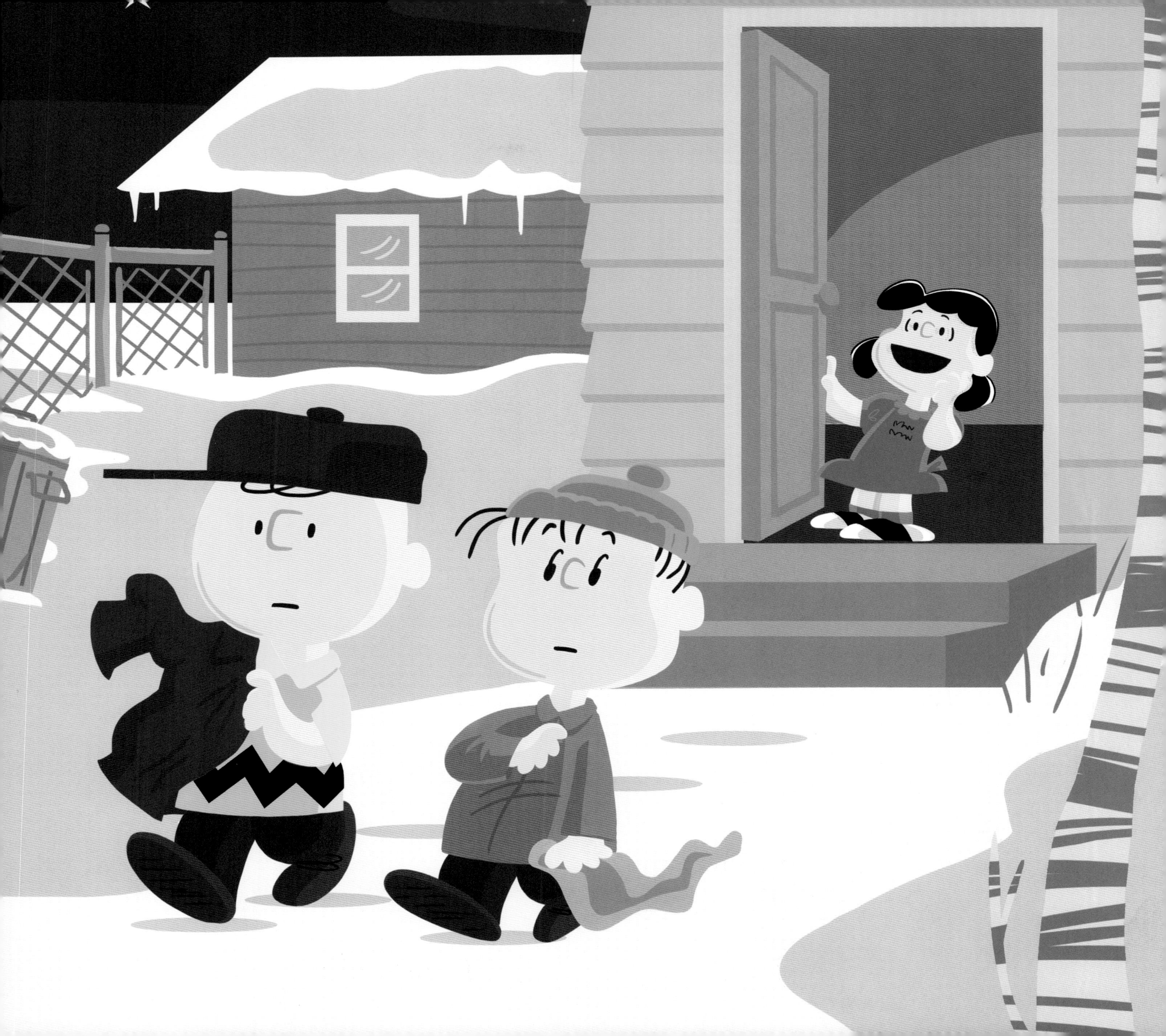

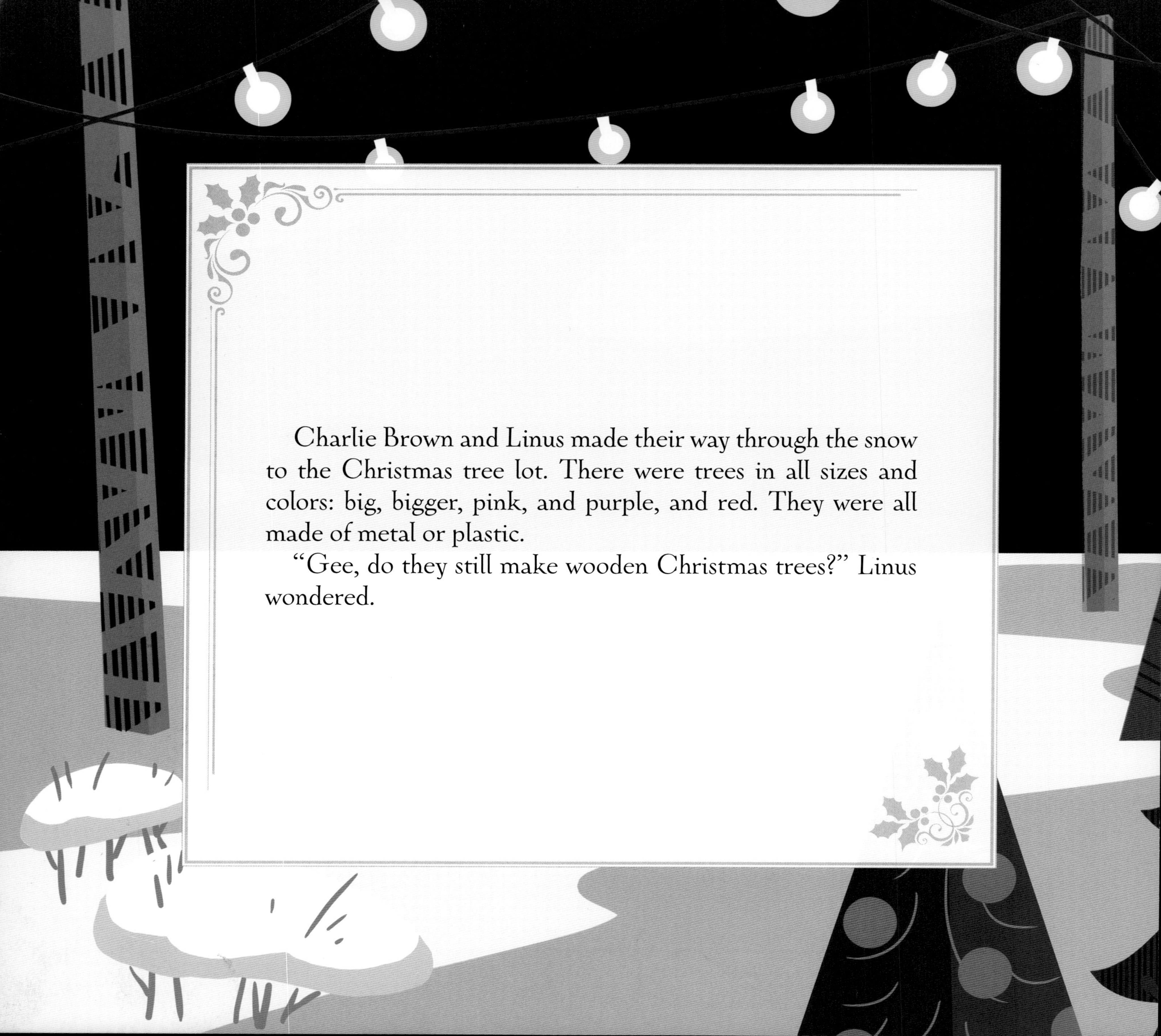

Charlie Brown and Linus made their way through the snow to the Christmas tree lot. There were trees in all sizes and colors: big, bigger, pink, and purple, and red. They were all made of metal or plastic.

"Gee, do they still make wooden Christmas trees?" Linus wondered.

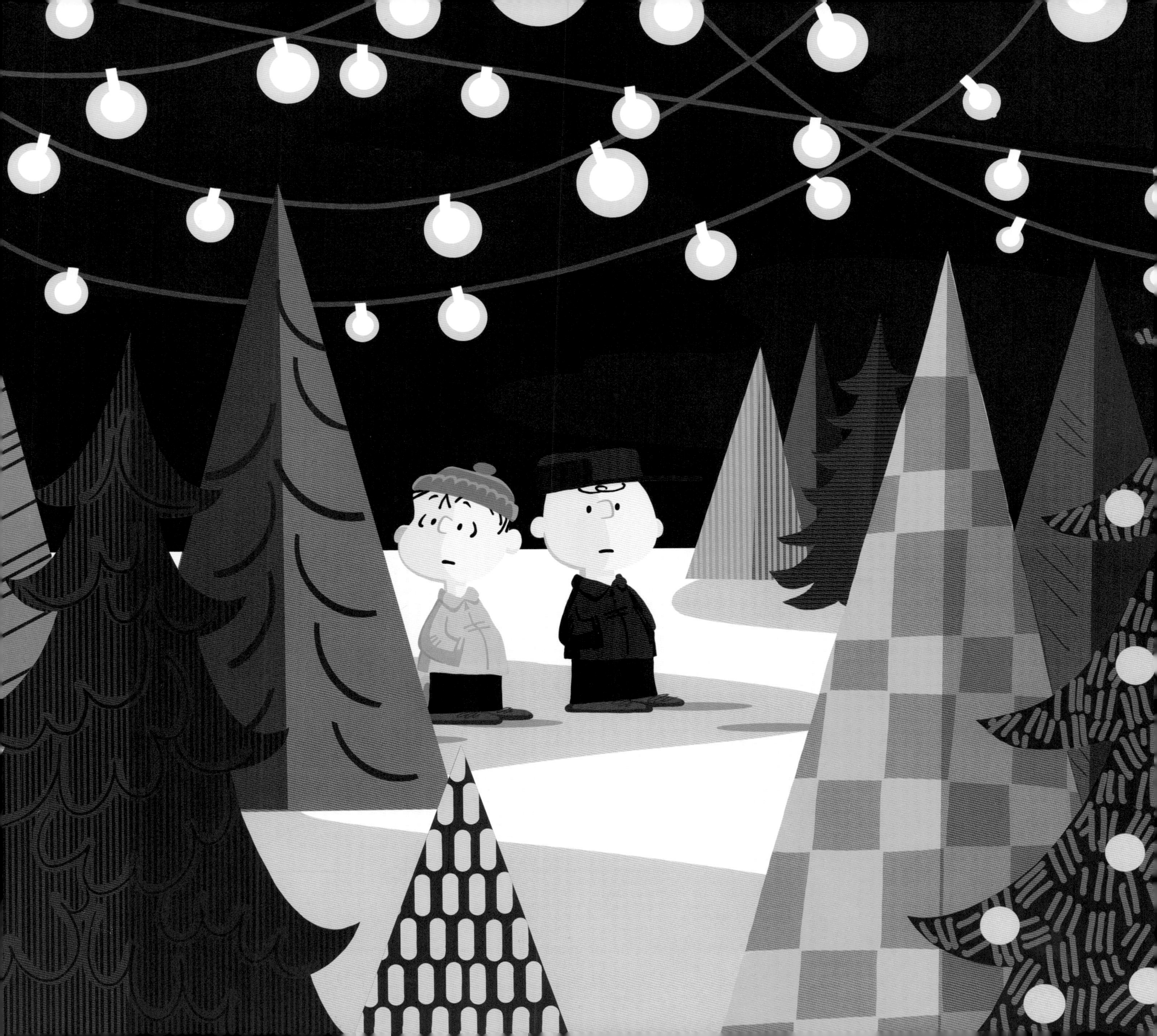

And that's when Charlie Brown saw it—the perfect Christmas tree.

"This little green one here seems to need a home," said Charlie Brown.

But Linus wasn't so sure. "I don't know, Charlie Brown. Remember what Lucy said? This doesn't seem to fit the modern spirit."

"I don't care," Charlie Brown said. "We'll decorate it, and it will be just right for our play. Besides, I think it needs me."

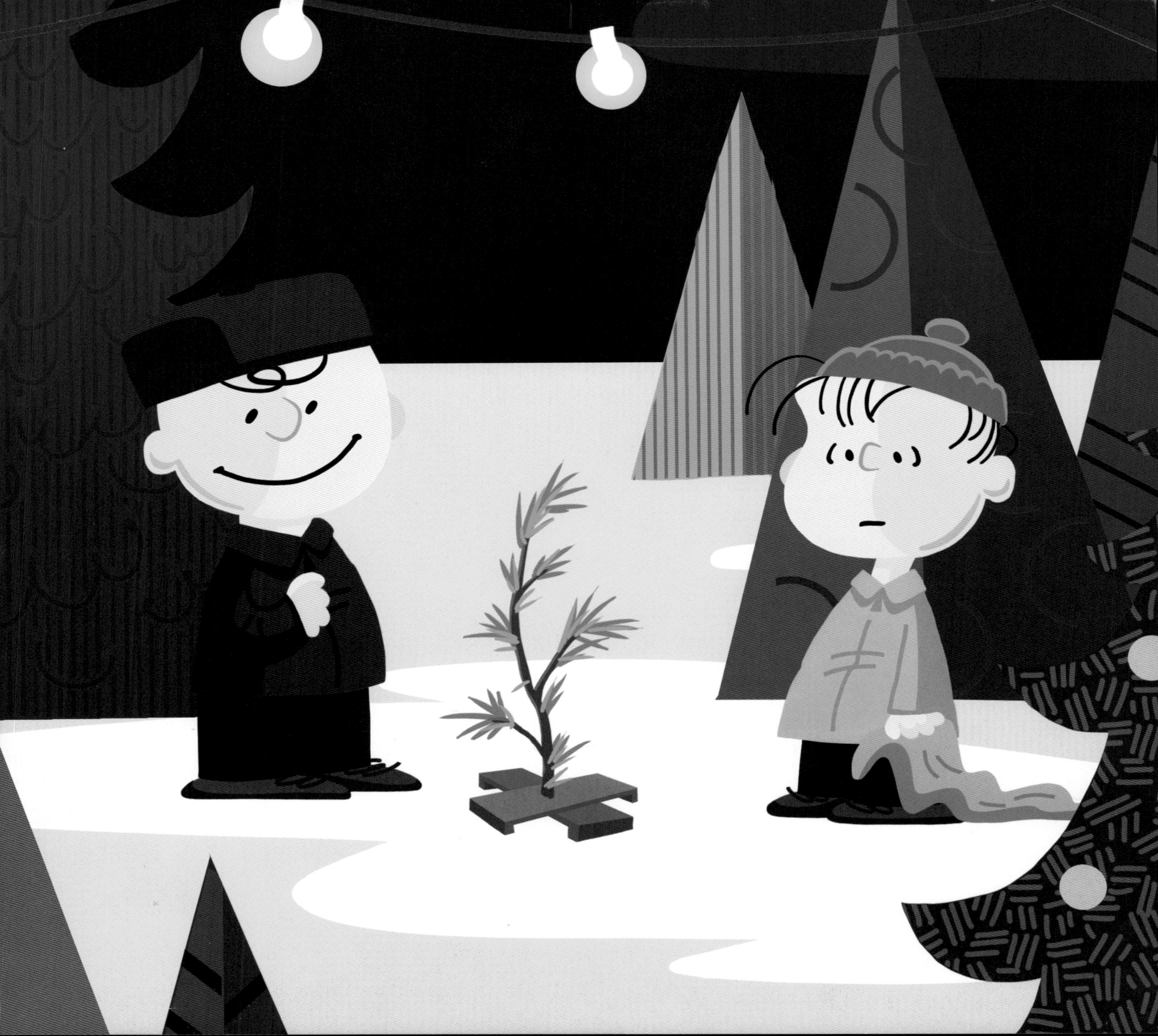

"We're back," Charlie Brown announced as he and Linus brought the little tree into the auditorium.

The other kids couldn't believe what they were seeing. This tree was all wrong!

"You were supposed to get a *good* tree," Lucy told Charlie Brown. "Can't you even tell a good tree from a poor tree?"

Everyone laughed and walked away—everyone except Linus.

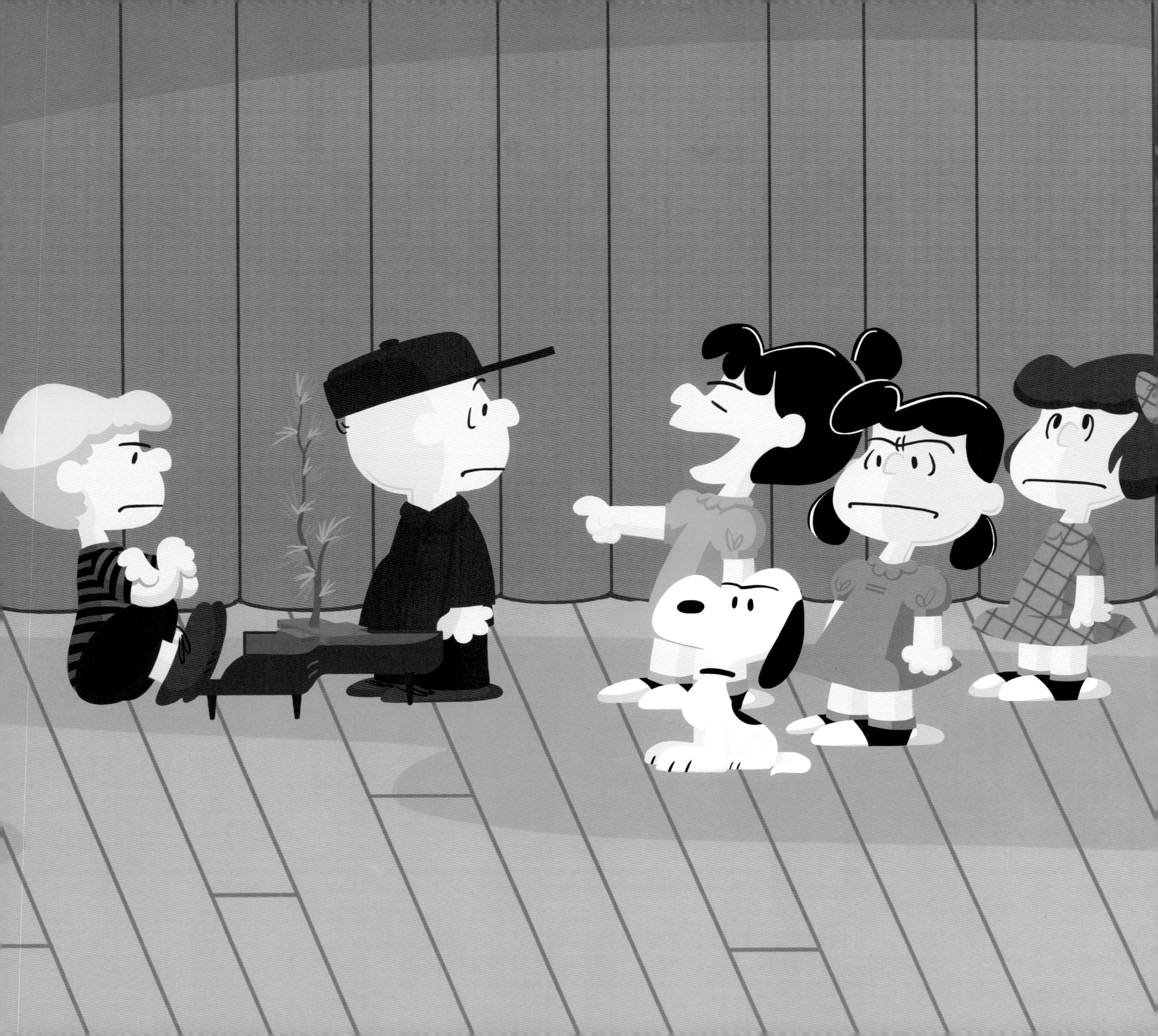

Charlie Brown turned to his friend. "I guess you were right, Linus. I shouldn't have picked this little tree. Everything I do turns into a disaster. I guess I really don't know what Christmas is all about. Isn't there anyone who knows what Christmas is all about?"

"Sure, Charlie Brown," said Linus. "I can tell you what Christmas is all about."

Linus walked to the center of the stage. A lone spotlight shone on him as he began to speak.

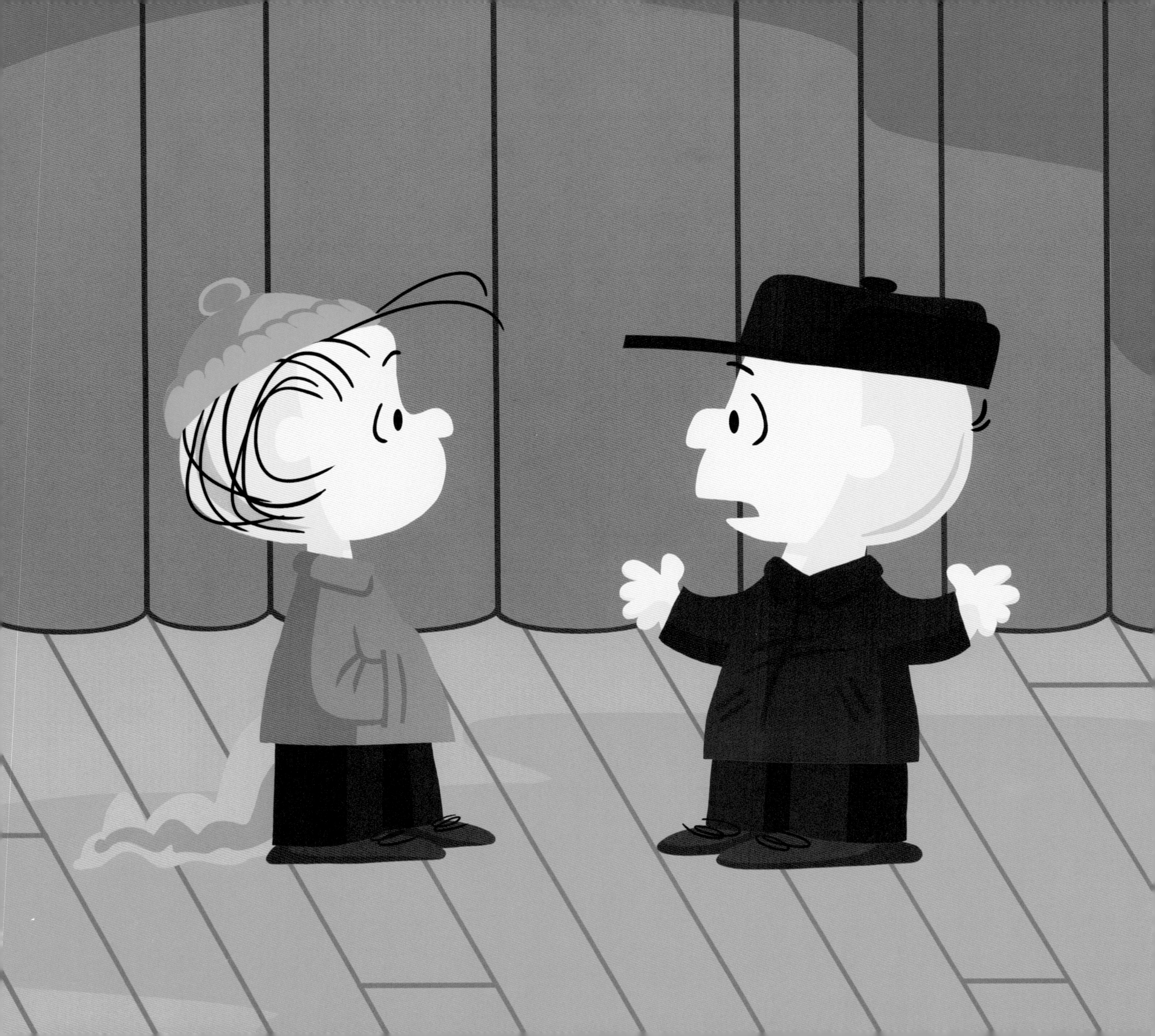

"And there were in the same country shepherds abiding in the field, keeping watch over their flock by night. And lo, the angel of the Lord came upon them, and the glory of the Lord shone round about them. And they were sore afraid. And the angel said unto them, 'Fear not, for behold, I bring you tidings of great joy, which will be to all people. For unto you is born this day in the city of David a Savior, which is Christ the Lord. And this shall be a sign unto you. Ye shall find the babe wrapped in swaddling clothes lying in a manger.' And suddenly there was with the angel a multitude of the heavenly host, praising God and saying, 'Glory to God in the highest, and on Earth peace, goodwill toward men.'"

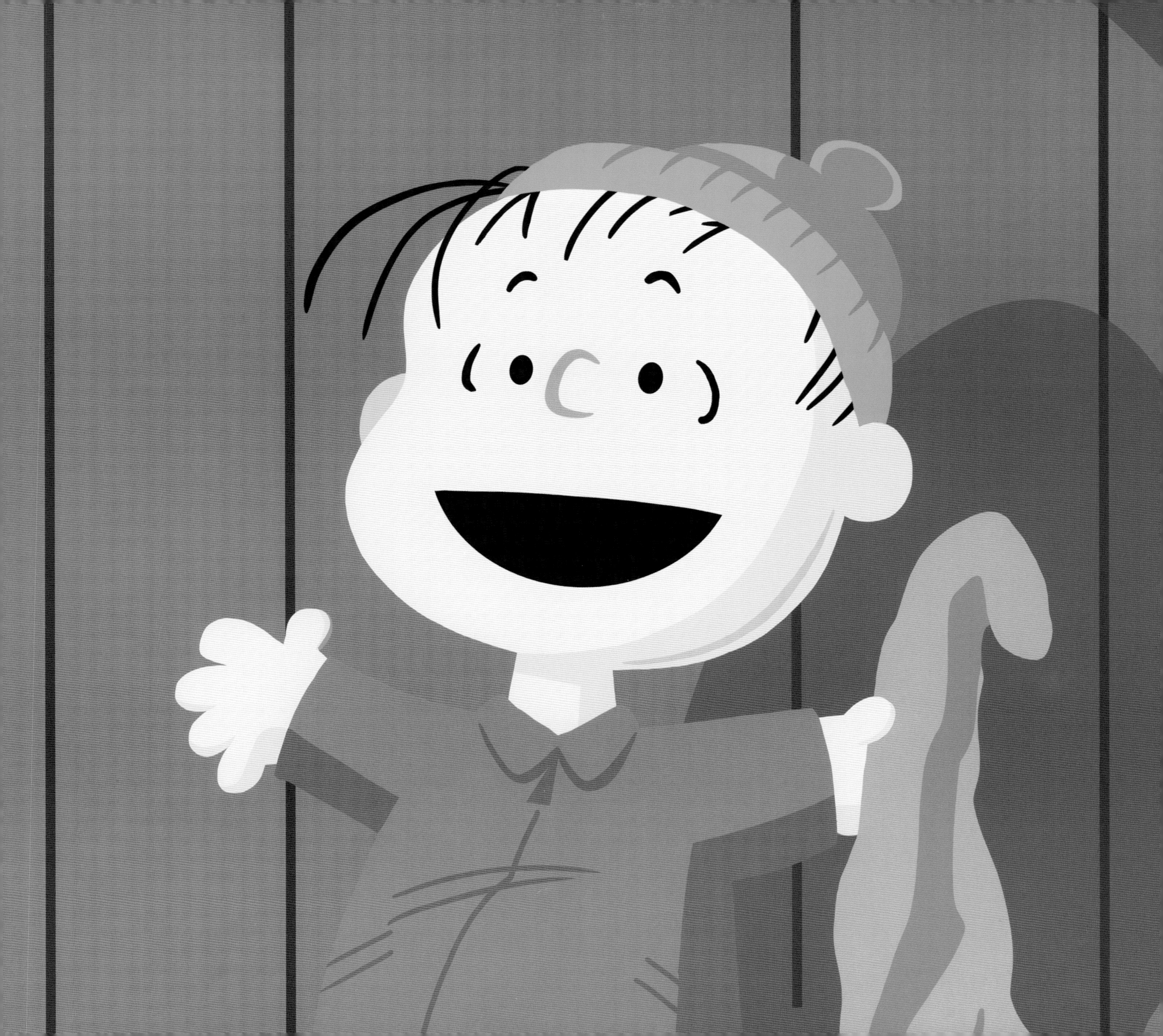

There was silence in the auditorium as Linus walked back to Charlie Brown. "That's what Christmas is all about, Charlie Brown," he added.

Charlie Brown thought about what Linus had said. He picked up the little tree and walked out of the auditorium.

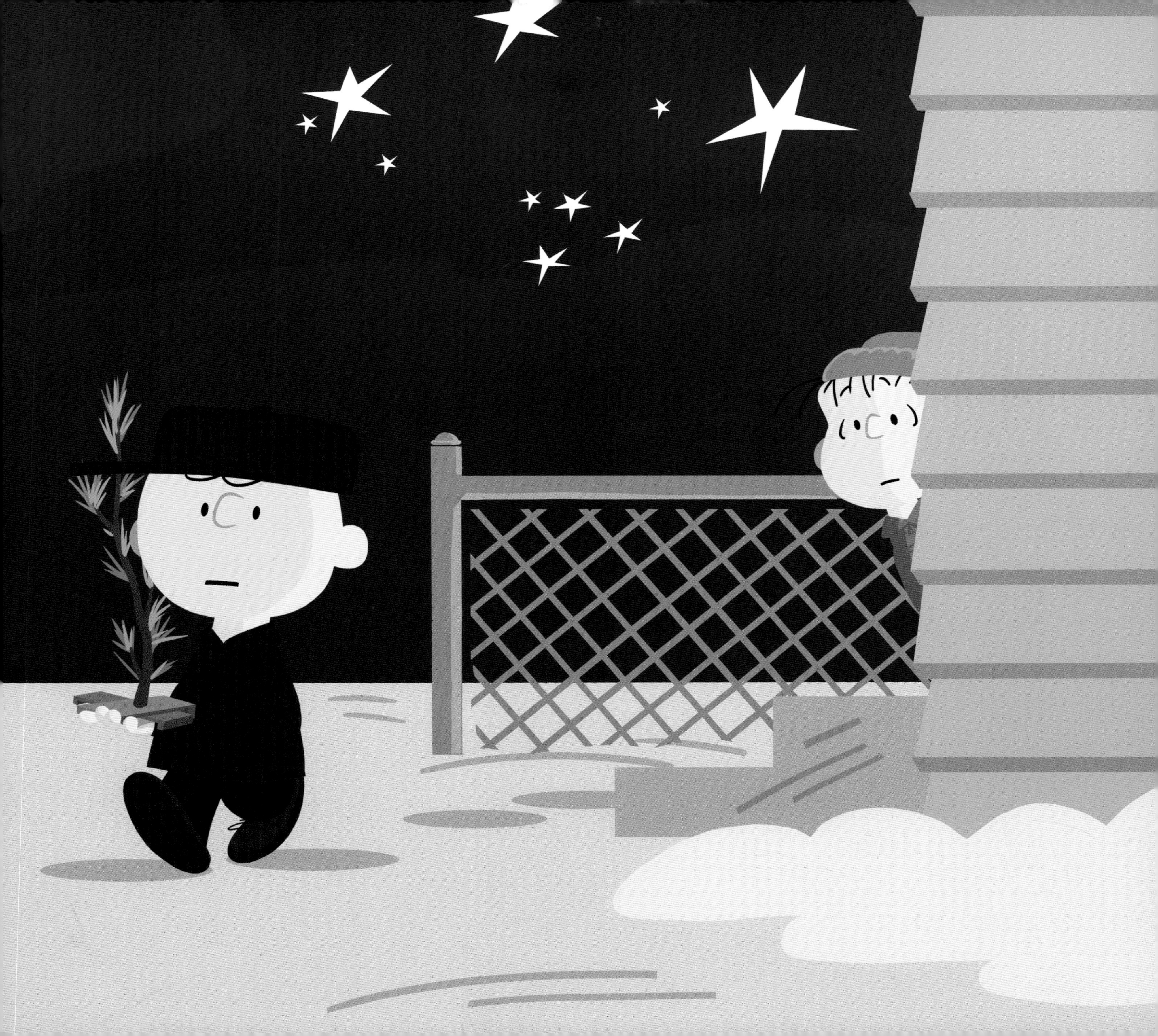

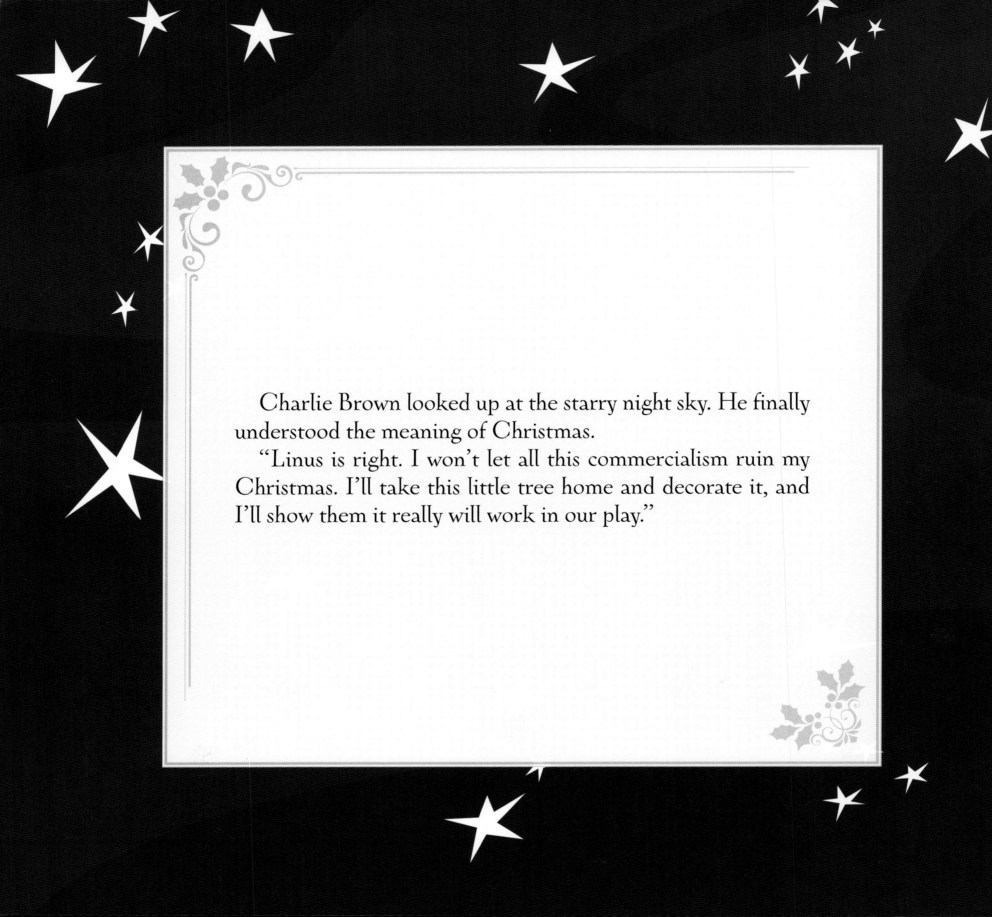

Charlie Brown looked up at the starry night sky. He finally understood the meaning of Christmas.

"Linus is right. I won't let all this commercialism ruin my Christmas. I'll take this little tree home and decorate it, and I'll show them it really will work in our play."

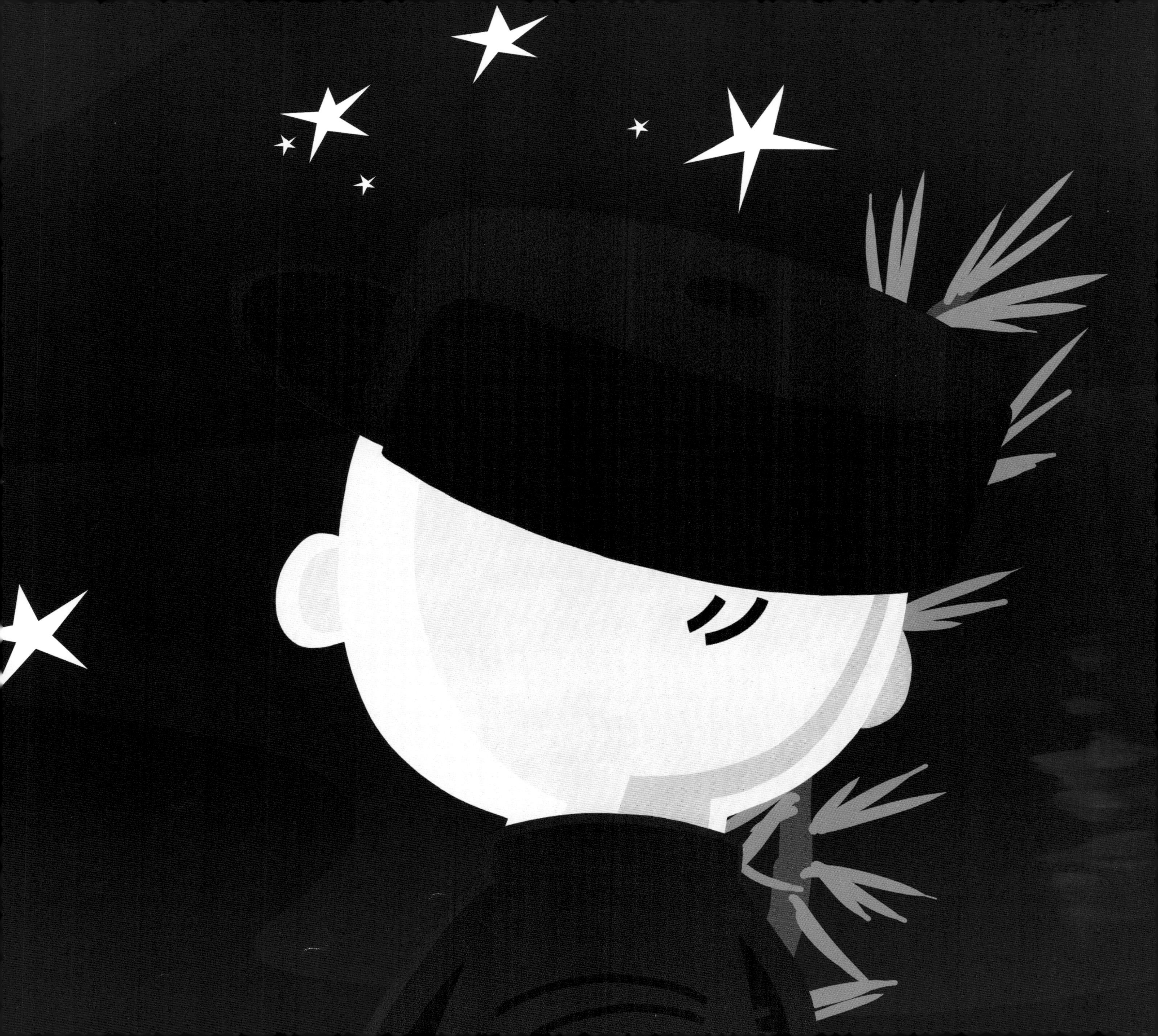

Charlie Brown took his tree to a place where he knew there would be a lot of decorations: Snoopy's doghouse. He selected a shiny red ornament. But when Charlie Brown put the ornament on the tree, it collapsed!

"I've killed it!" Charlie Brown cried. "Everything I touch gets ruined!"

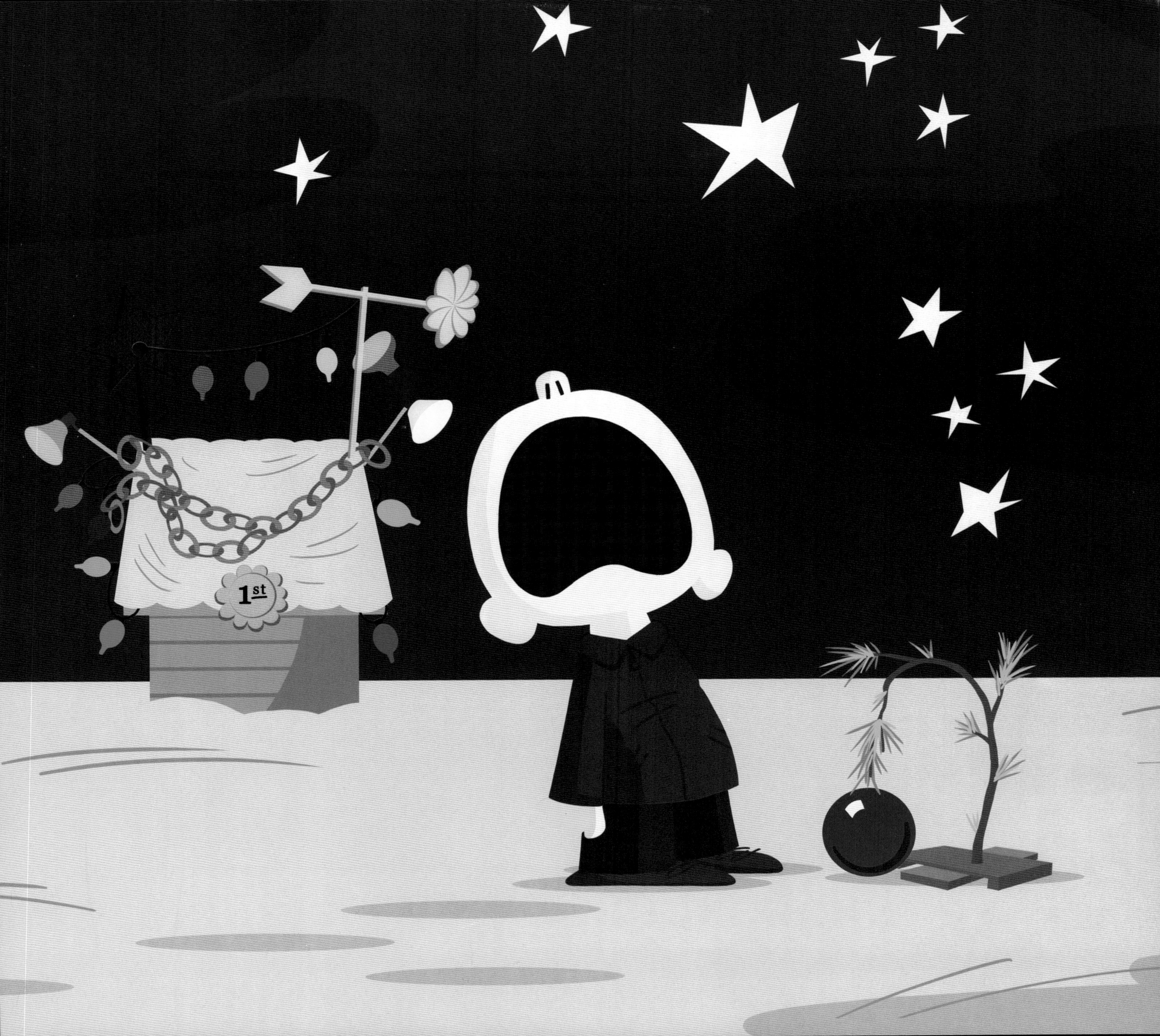
1st

Charlie Brown walked off in despair. A few moments later, the other children arrived.

"I never thought it was such a bad little tree," Linus said as he wrapped his blanket around its base. "It's not bad at all, really. Maybe it just needs a little love."

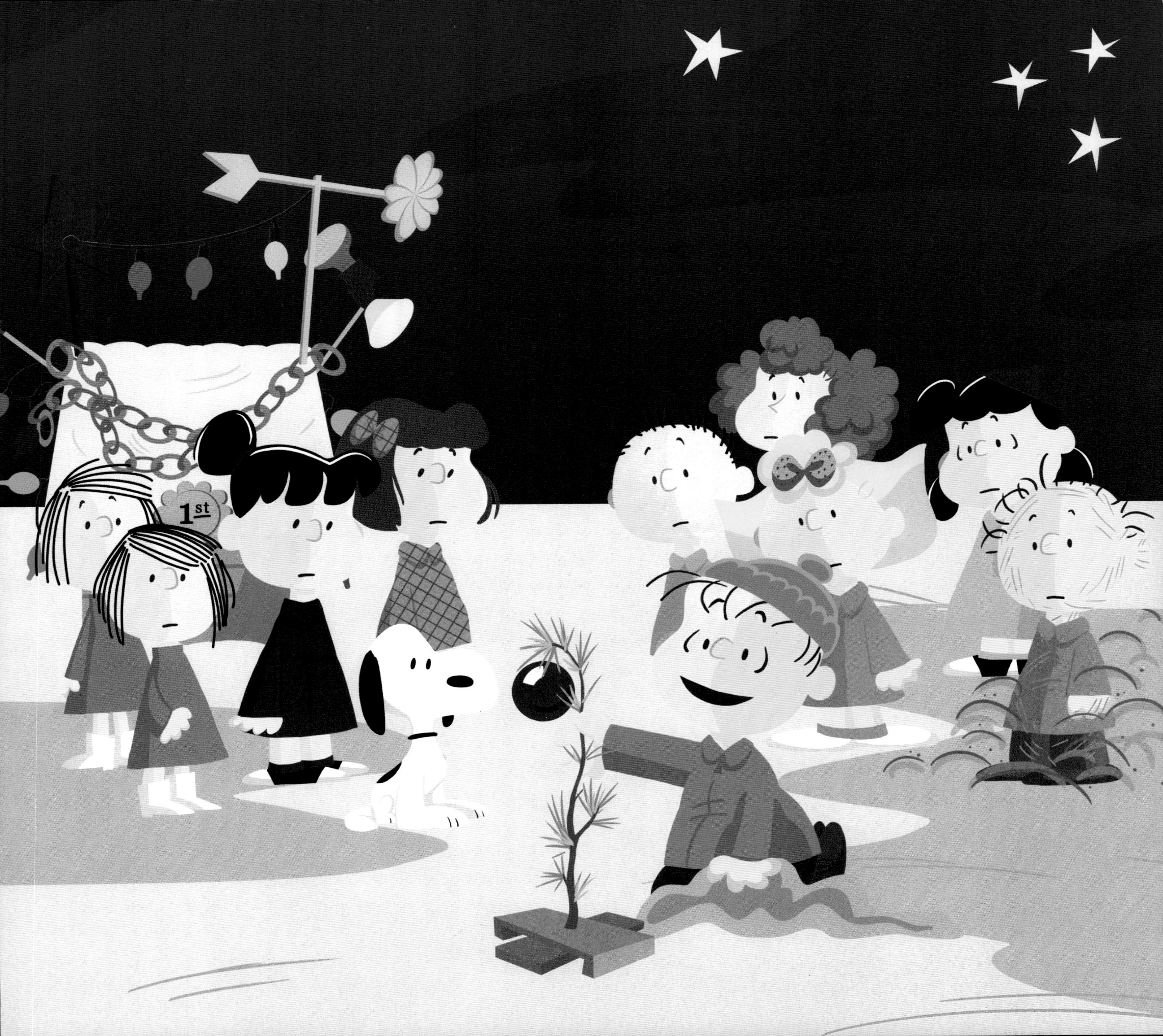
1st

Everyone began taking ornaments off Snoopy's doghouse. Soon, the little tree had been transformed into a festive Christmas tree.

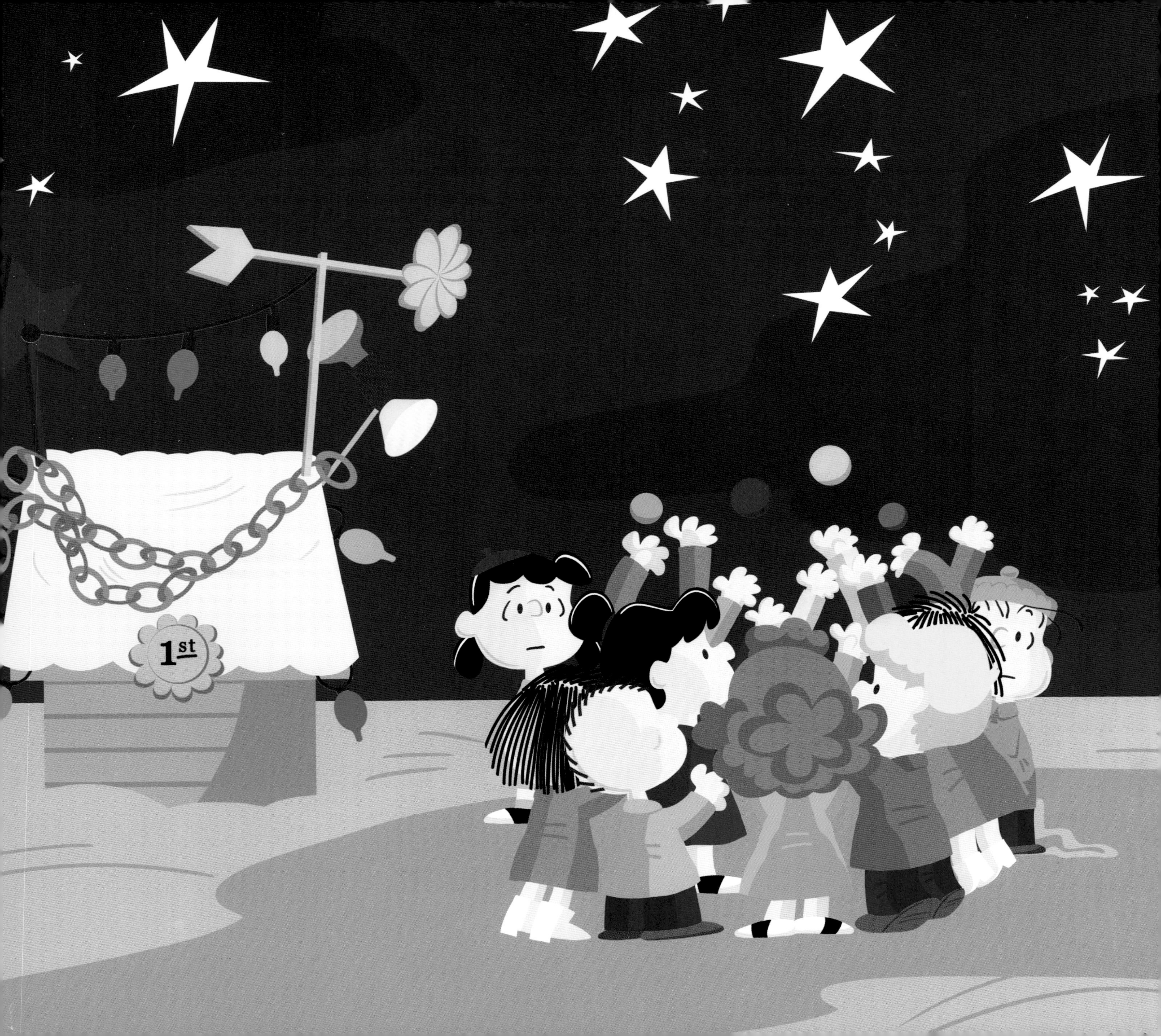
1st

When Charlie Brown returned, he was stunned. "What's going on here?" he asked.

"Merry Christmas, Charlie Brown!" all the kids said.

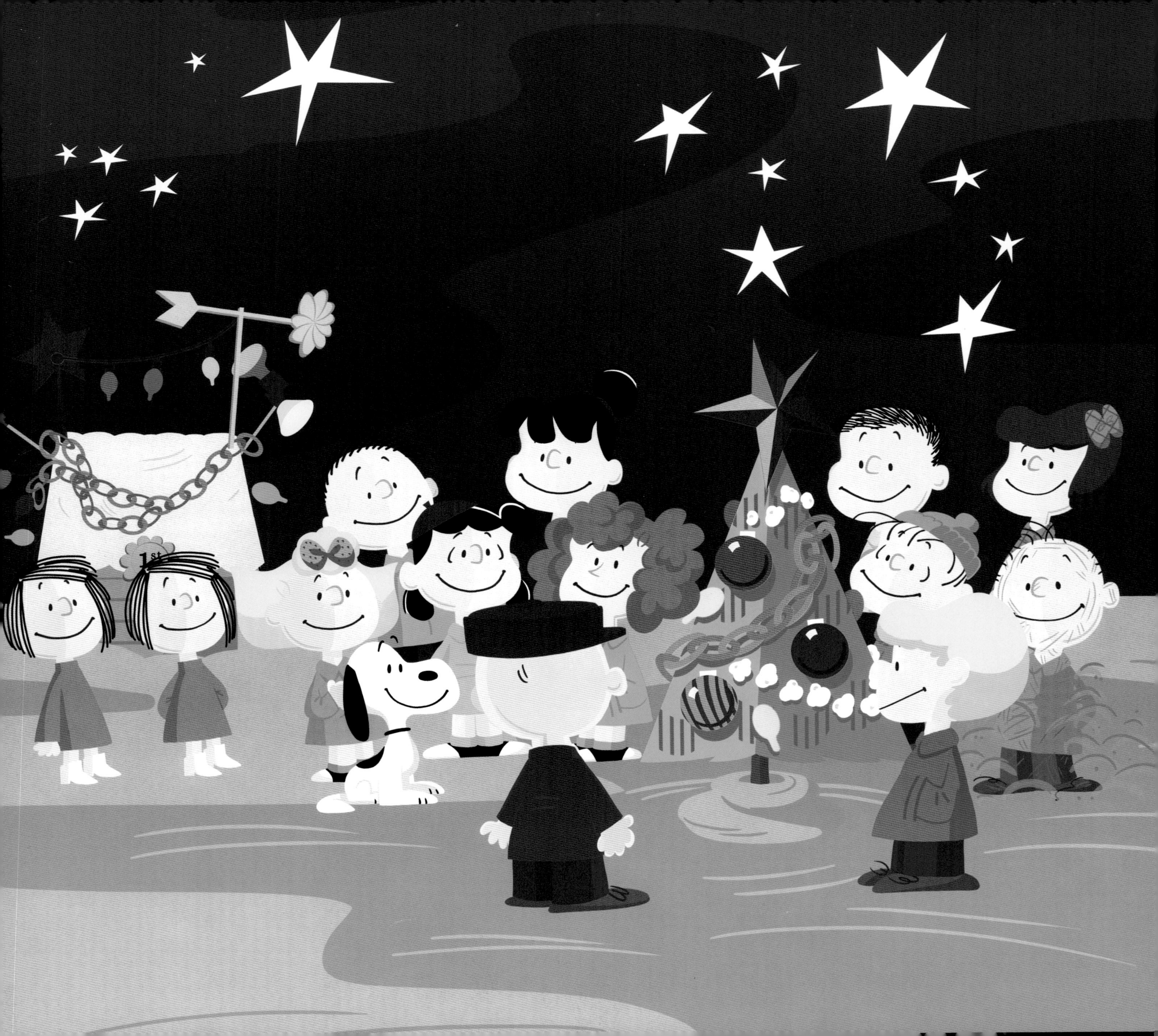
1st

And then everyone began to sing—even Charlie Brown.

Hark! The herald angels sing,
"Glory to the newborn King!
Peace on Earth and mercy mild,
God and sinners reconciled."
Joyful, all ye nations, rise,
Join the triumph of the skies,
With angelic host proclaim:
"Christ is born in Bethlehem."
Hark! The herald angels sing,
"Glory to the newborn King!"

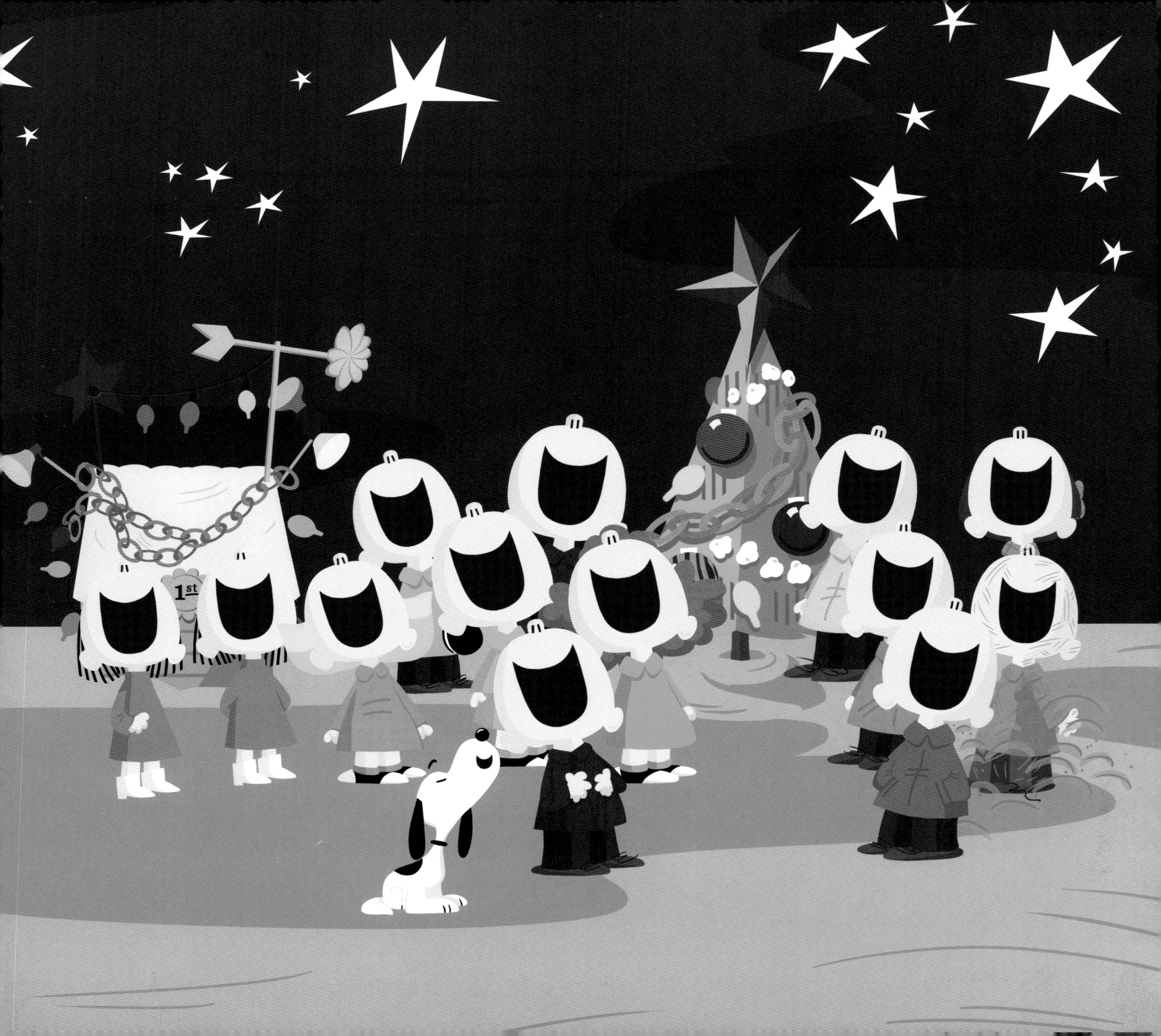
1st

THE END

HARK! THE HERALD ANGELS SING

FELIX MENDELSSOHN

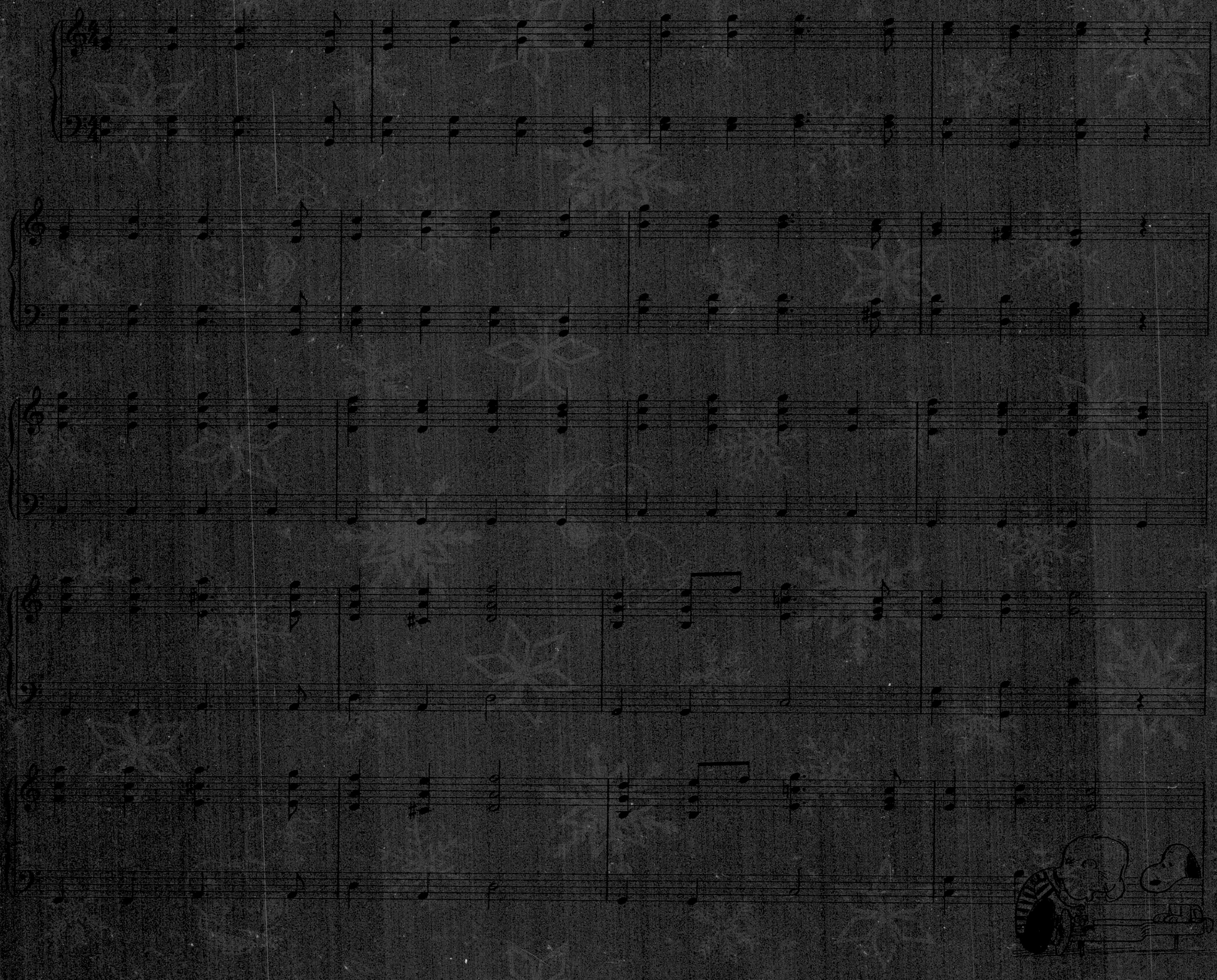